This series is dedicated to my family, and all military families, for their unwavering support, their infinite love, and their sacrifice for our country.

- Johnathan Edmonds

www.mascotbooks.com

©2013 AJE Ventures, LLC. All Rights Reserved.
No part of this publication may be reproduced, stored in a
retrieval system or transmitted in any form by any means
electronic, mechanical, or photocopying, recording or otherwise
without the permission of the author.

For more information, please contact:
Mascot Books
560 Herndon Parkway #120
Herndon, VA 20170
info@mascotbooks.com

Library of Congress Control Number: 2012952880

PRT0113A
ISBN-10: 1620861569
ISBN-13: 9781620861561

Printed in the United States

MARINE

SERVICE PALS™

IN
★ THE HONOR RELAY ★

JOHNATHAN EDMONDS

ILLUSTRATED BY
ADAM SCHARTUP

Wiley Wendy Wrecker was sitting in her garage as she watched the members of the Marine Service Pals training for the upcoming Honor Relay, a race through the water, in the air, and across land. She was sad because this was the first year she didn't make the relay team.

The Service Pals
Team was stacked
with talent and they
were going to need it. The
Foreign Corps, an undefeated team,
was coming to town for the first time. There
was Hasty Holly Hornet practicing her speedy
flight across the sky. Her engines were screaming
and she was moving as fast as lightning.

There was Outgoing Opal Osprey practicing her landings on a dime. Her blades were going *woop, woop, woop, woop, woop.*

In the water, there was Gutsy Gabby Gator. She went in and out of the water as quick as a wink.

Proud Perry Patroller was busy sliding across the water.

Over in the sand was the highly decorated
Honorable Henry Humvee playing around.

Finally, there was Trucking Tucker Truck who was pulling a heavy load.

As Trucking Tucker passed by, he saw Wiley Wendy who had wandered over to the airstrip.

"Hi, Wiley Wendy. Sorry you did not make the team this year," he said.

Wiley Wendy smiled, "Thanks. I hope you guys beat the Foreign Corps this weekend."

Just then, Hasty Holly landed and, boy, was she sweating!

"How was your flight, Holly?" Wiley Wendy asked.

"It was great!" Hasty Holly replied. "I just hope we beat the Foreign Corps. They are the best in the world, you know."

The next day, the Foreign Corps team arrived in town. As they passed by, Wiley Wendy noticed how big and strong they were. They sure looked like the best in the world.

As race time approached, crowds began to fill the stands. Even Handsome Holden Hornet and Steady Stacy Seahawk from the Navy Service Pals had flown in to watch the relay. The spectators noticed how big and strong the other team looked.

"Wow, the Marine Service Pals have no chance to win!" one child exclaimed.

The racers started warming up,
when all of a sudden...

BANG!

Trucking Tucker had blown his engine!

"Oh no!" everyone cried. The Marine Service Pals couldn't believe it. Someone had to fill Trucking Tucker's place.

Out of nowhere, Wiley Wendy piped up, "I am a Marine Service Pal and I can do it!"

"Yes, you are," said Honorable Henry, "and you can join the relay."

Wiley Wendy was so excited! She went right to her position.

BANG!

With the shot of a gun, the race was on. Proud Perry was off like a rocket but he was neck and neck with the other team's boat as they flew across the water.

RACE START

Bam! Proud Perry made the handoff to Gutsy Gabby.

She went in and out of the water and over and around the obstacles. Gutsy Gabby was slow, but managed to keep up with the other team.

Gutsy Gabby was quickly approaching Outgoing Opal and finally made it to her. Tag!

Outgoing Opal lifted into the air. She had to maneuver through hoops, around clouds, and sidestep birds until Hasty Holly appeared. As she tagged Hasty Holly, she noticed the other team starting to pull ahead.

Hasty Holly pushed the throttle up and streaked across the sky. Slowly but surely, she caught up to the other team.

As she came in for a landing, Honorable Henry was waiting to receive the tag. As soon as Hasty Holly tagged Honorable Henry, he started weaving in and out of the trees, over the wall, into the tunnel, and over the hill.

He lost track of the other team because they were pulling away. He finally reached Wiley Wendy.

She was hooked up to her load and could barely see the other team in the distance as she received the tag. Wiley Wendy zoomed away, knowing she didn't have much time to catch up. Little by little, she caught up to the other team, pulling harder and harder as each second passed.

The finish line was in sight! She kept saying over and over to herself, "I am a Marine Service Pal. I can do it!"

"You can do it, Wiley Wendy! You're a Marine Service Pal!" yelled Honorable Henry.

As she crossed the finish line, she looked up to the scoreboard and saw that she had done it. She won the race!

The crowd went wild! The Marine Service Pals had beaten the best relay team in the world!

"Great job, Wiley Wendy!" exclaimed the rest of the relay team. They were waiting for her at the finish line.

"You won the race for us, Wiley Wendy," said Trucking Tucker. "You definitely deserved to be in my place."

"Thanks, everyone," said Wiley Wendy. "But I didn't win the race alone. We won as a team because we, the Marine Service Pals, can do anything!"

THE END

LEARN MORE ABOUT THE
MARINE
SERVICE PALS ™

Hasty Holly Hornet is a fighter jet. She can go very fast and has 2 engines. She usually has ▶ 1 pilot, but sometimes may have 2.

Outgoing Opal Osprey is a vertical takeoff ◀ plane. She has 2 turbo prop engines. She can carry 24 people or 20,000 pounds of cargo.

Honorable Henry Humvee is a 4-wheel drive, all-purpose vehicle. He can serve as a transport vehicle, radar station, ▶ or ambulance. He has a top speed of over 70 mph.

Gutsy Gabby Gator is known as an amphibious tractor, ◀ or a truck that can travel in the water as well as on land. She can travel at 5 mph in the water and 45 mph on land.

Trucking Tucker Truck is a 6-wheel drive truck. He is affectionately called the "7 Ton" for the amount of weight he can carry. He is considered ▶ the prime mover for the Marine Service Pals.

Proud Perry Patroller is a patrol boat. He is known for ◀ scouting, medical transport, and resupply operations. He can travel at 35 mph and has 2 diesel engines.

Wiley Wendy Wrecker is an 8-wheel drive truck who can carry 25,000 pounds off road. She can also be fitted to serve as a flatbed truck or medical care facility.

Howling Howard Harrier is a fighter jet. He is known as a "Jump Jet" and can take off ▶ by lifting straight up. He has 2 jet engines.

Mighty Maddie Marine One is a helicopter that is most known for carrying the President of the United States. She has 1 rotor and can travel at 166 mph.

Intense Indy Intruder is a jet aircraft. Although he is retired, he is still very strong. He can travel at 640 mph. He also can carry fuel to transfer to other airplanes.

Strong Stanley Stallion is a super heavy-duty lift helicopter. He has 1 rotor with 5 blades powered by 2 engines. He can carry 8,000 pounds of cargo at 170 mph.

Sporty Sawyer Skids is a Cobra helicopter. He has 2 crew members and 1 main rotor. ▶ He can travel at 145 mph.

COLLECT ALL OF THE BOOKS IN THE

SERIES

AIR FORCE SERVICE PALS IN THE AMAZING AIRSHOW

MARINE SERVICE PALS IN THE HONOR RELAY

ARMY SERVICE PALS SEARCH FOR SERGEANT MIKE

NAVY SERVICE PALS TRAVEL AROUND THE WORLD

ABOUT THE AUTHOR

Johnathan Edmonds, a sixteen-year veteran of the US Navy and US Air Force, grew up in Blain, Pennsylvania. At the age of eighteen, he enlisted in the US Navy as an Aviation Electronics Technician. After being honorably discharged, he studied computer engineering at Virginia Tech. Upon receiving his Bachelor's degree, Johnathan began his computer engineering career and soon joined the US Air Force Reserves, fulfilling his lifelong desire to fly planes. He also earned a Master's degree from North Carolina State University in computer engineering. He resides with his family near Raleigh, North Carolina.

To learn more about Johnathan and the Service Pals, please visit www.myservicepals.com.